WILD LOVE

WILD HEART MOUNTAIN: WILD RIDERS MC
BOOK NINE

SADIE KING

WILD RIDERS MC

AN INTRODUCTION

Welcome to Wild Heart Mountain home of the Wild Riders MC.

If you love damaged heroes and curvy girl romance, then you'll love the Wild Riders MC.

This group of ex-military bikers fall hard and fall fast when they encounter the curvy women who heal their hearts.

Expect forbidden love, age gap, forced proximity, fake relationships, single dads, single moms and off-limits love with protective heroes who will do anything for the women they love.

Spend some time with Wild Heart Mountain's Wild Riders MC, the MC that's all heart.

Let me introduce you to the members…

Ex-military buddies **Raiden, Quentin and Travis** formed the Wild Riders MC when they got out of the military and wanted to create a place for veterans who love to ride.

They set up their headquarters in a compound on the side of Wild Heart Mountain.

Travis, whose road name is Hops, runs the Wild Taste Bar and Restaurant, and secretly crushes on his best friend's sister.

Quentin, also known as Barrels, runs the award-winning Wild Taste Brewery located out the back of the restaurant. He was a First Class Sargent in the army and you wouldn't want to cross him. Especially where his little sister is concerned...

Colter, or Vintage, is a motorbike mechanic and runs the bike shop. He collects old bikes and loves all things vintage especially the bubbly Danni and her 1950's curves.

Calvin also known as Badge, is the local Sheriff and his uptight views that are shaped by loss.

Joseph, or Lone Star is a recluse whose military experiences have given him a distaste for humanity.

Grant goes by Snips. He's the local barber and a single dad.

Arlo earns the road name Prince because of his charming and personable nature. He loves getting under the skin of Maggie, the shy pastry chef.

Davis begins the series as a prospect. Younger than most of the other men, he came out of the military with diminished hearing. His hearing aids keeps make him shy with women and he keeps himself hidden away.

Luke becomes a prospect after Raiden finds him drinking himself to oblivion in a strip joint. A wheelchair user since he lost both his legs in Afghanistan, Luke finds new purpose with the MC, but can he find love?

Specs would rather read a book than talk to anyone.

Bit Rate is a grumpy single dad widower in need of a nanny.

Judge is a military lawyer and always does the right thing until he meets the curvy woman who makes him question his world view.

Marcus goes by Wood because his family own the local sawmill and it's his medium of choice. He channels his PTSD into his art, creating sculptures that attract the attention of an arts journalist from the city.

On the other side of Wild Heart Mountain is a town called Hope and nestled in the hills is the Emerald Heart

Resort. During the summer, it's a popular destination for tourists and in winter, they come for the ski season. Perfect for a snowed in romance...

Stay awhile in Wild Heart Mountain and explore the other series set here.

Wild Heart Mountain: Military Heroes
Wild Heart Mountain: Mountain Heroes
Temptation
A Runaway Bride for Christmas
A Secret Baby for Christmas

WILD LOVE

WILD RIDERS MC

He's a wounded ex-soldier, and she's the older woman who's off limits...

Mel's confident and smart with curves for days. But there's no way this sophisticated city girl would want a damaged veteran like me. I'm rough around the edges, damaged from the military, and working as a bartender for the Wild Riders MC.

I'm a bearded, tattooed biker and she's used to suave city men. There's no way I even stand a chance.

Until she climbs into my bed and takes control, taking what she needs from me and driving me wild.

When Mel goes back to the city, she takes a part of me with her, and I find out how far I'm prepared to go for this wild love.

Wild Love is Davis and Mel's story, a steamy instalove OW/YM romance featuring an ex-military hero and the curvy woman he falls hard for.

DAVIS

*I*t's a crisp morning as I pull into the parking lot of the Wild Riders Motorcycle Club. I park my Harley by the workshop, making sure to tuck the sidecar in and allow room for the rest of the bikes which will turn up later in the day. Hercules licks my hand as I slide off the bike, impatient this morning to get out of the sidecar.

I slip my helmet off and insert my hearing aids. There's a moment of feedback that makes me wince before the sounds of the morning form clear and sharp in my ears.

Across the parking lot, Danni is getting out of her Cadillac with a duffel bag that she hands to Badge. He's with Grace, the woman I met yesterday, although she's ditched the wedding dress. I don't know what the story is with her. I'll have to ask Badge later.

Someone else gets out of the passenger's side of the Caddy and Hercules whines.

I take his goggles off and unclip his harness.

As I'm grabbing my gear out of the saddle bag, Hercules vaults out of the sidecar with an excited yelp.

He's a strong and solid St Bernard and usually far too lazy to get excited about anything. I turn to see what's got his attention but he's already careening across the parking lot.

"Hercules!"

He's gone before I can grab him, a happy bark the only warning before he plunges into the group of people standing around Danni's Caddy.

I race after him and hear a female screech. He's got his paws up on someone, and by the time I reach him he's pushed the poor woman backwards till she's leaning against the door of the Caddy with Hercules's paws on her white shirt, boxing her in.

"Hercules, get down!"

The big animal has his tongue hanging out in a silly doggy grin and is about to drool all over the woman's no longer white shirt.

"I'm so sorry." I tug on Hercules's collar. "He's never done anything…"

As I pull Hercules away, my eyes travel up the woman's body, from her tight-fitting blouse showing off generous curves to the shocked pink mouth and brown eyes wide with surprise. Her dark hair falls over her shoulders and a breeze catches it, making the tendrils swirl like chocolate.

Her eyes meet mine, dark as the woods at twilight.

My mouth goes dry, and my mind blank.

I stare at the woman in front of me, not able to break the eye contact.

Hercules gives my hand a slobbery lick and whines, but I can't take my eyes off the beauty before me.

"It's okay." She looks down at the muddy prints staining her shirt. "It's only a shirt…" Her lip trembles and she blinks quickly, her voice wavering. "Only an Armani shirt…"

"Oh no," Danni mutters.

I watch in horror as tears spill from the corners of the woman's eyes. The most beautiful woman I've ever seen, and I've made her cry.

"I'm so sorry."

Damn Hercules. He's on half rations for this. "I didn't mean to upset you."

Danni slides an arm around the woman's shoulders.

"It's not you, sweetie," she says to me. "Mel's going through…a hard time."

Mel. The goddess is called Mel. Standing together, I see the resemblance. Danni's got her hair pinned up and her customary red lipstick, but they have the same shaped face, the same color hair and full lips.

This must be Mel, her sister who I've heard her talk about. The big sister from the city. Her sister who's now crying because my big beautiful dumb dog scared the hell out of her and ruined her Armani blouse.

I watch her walk away, enjoying the sway of her generous hips.

"Nice one, Hercules," I mutter as Danni leads the tearful Mel into the clubhouse.

2

MEL

*D*anni leads me through a door and down a corridor to an office. She closes the door behind me, giving us privacy, and I lean against my sister and let the emotion from the past twenty-four hours roll out of me.

"Hush." She runs her hands over my hair, whispering soothing sounds the way I've heard her do with her kids.

The switch in our positions is not lost on me. I'm the big sister who always had her shit together, but today it's my little sister who's comforting me, and I'm the one who's a blubbering hot mess.

"It's okay," Danni coos in her soothing voice. "You're better off without him, Mel."

There's a box of tissues on the desk, and Danni hands me one. I give my nose a honking blow and take another tissue to dab at my eyes.

"I know I'm better off without him. It's just…"

I sigh deeply, not sure what it is I'm feeling. Twelve

hours ago I walked out of my office, where my asshole of an ex also works, and I didn't go home. I took a bus to the train station and bought a one way ticket to Hope, the closest town to Danni with a station.

She picked me up at the other end with no questions.

It was my decision to leave Jeff and long overdue. I'm not crying for Jeff; I'm crying because it's been a long-ass twenty-four hours. My career may be ruined, I've got nowhere to live, I'm tired from trying to sleep on Danni's couch, and I've got a video call in thirty minutes and my favorite shirt is streaked with mud.

"I've got nothing to wear for my meeting."

I glance down at the streaks of dirt on my favorite shirt, the Armani that I treated myself to on my last birthday because Jeff forgot to get me anything.

I feel like a boss whenever I wear this shirt. Like I'm in control and a badass. But that confidence disappeared somewhere overnight while putting my neck out on Danni's couch and questioning my spontaneous decision to leave without so much as a change of underwear.

But after Jeff humiliated me at work yesterday, it was the final straw. The only safe place I could go was to my sister's. I didn't realize they were in the middle of a renovation, extending the cabin to fit their growing family.

Danni insists I stay, but the WiFi at their cabin is patchy and it's noisy, so she brought me to the clubhouse today to work.

When my sister told me she'd hooked up with a guy from a motorcycle club, I was skeptical until I met Colter. They're a perfect match, and the MC is all veterans and they run legit businesses. They're ex-soldiers who like to ride.

Danni says it's the family she's never had, which I try not to take offense at. I take it she's referring to the acceptance she found here which she never got from our mom.

The thought of Mom makes me shudder. She's going to flip when I tell her I've left Jeff and the wedding's off. I was always her golden girl, but only because my life choices happened to align with what she thought I should do. Well, mostly.

I sigh, not wanting to think about Mom and my ex-fiancée.

"The Prez isn't here at the moment, but I'll speak to Barrels and tell him you'll be working here for the day," Danni says.

My brow furrows.

"Barrels?"

She grins. "Quentin. But they all have road names here, like a nickname."

I'll have to get used to that. "Who's the guy with the dog?"

After he pulled the giant thing off me, I was struck by the man with the shaggy hair and kind eyes.

"That's Davis. He works in the bar most days. You need anything, you just ask him."

I pat at my eyes and throw the tissues in the bin. I've got a meeting with my team, and after what Jeff did yesterday, the last thing I need is to look like I've been crying.

"You got a spare shirt I can borrow?"

Danni nods. "There'll be something around. I'll get you set up in the restaurant and see what I can find."

I follow Danni through to the restaurant and bar area.

Bike memorabilia adorns the walls, and there's an old Harley mounted in the corner. There's no mistaking it's a bikers bar, but it's classy. The kind of place that anyone would feel welcome in.

I take a table in the corner while Danni goes to find me a shirt.

I'm setting up my laptop when a shadow falls over the table. I glance up to find Davis holding a mug of something steamy.

"I'm so sorry about Hercules." He holds out the mug. "Coffee?"

His eyes are sea green which contrast with his dark hair that hangs over his ears. Rough stubble coats his chin, giving him a scruffy look. The leather jacket falls open to reveal a tight white t-shirt that clings to his torso. He's broad and big and more rugged than I imagined an ex-soldier to be.

I'm reminded of Jeff and his manicured hands and immaculate white shirts. I shudder and shake the image out of my head.

"It's okay."

I don't want him to think I was crying over a dirty shirt, but I'm not ready to share my situation with a stranger.

"It wasn't about the dog, honestly, and it's just a fucking shirt, right?"

7

I press my lips together, annoyed at myself for swearing. That's the city coming out in me. But I don't want to disrespect anyone in their clubhouse where I'm a guest, and I don't want this man to think I'm crass. I don't know why, but it seems important to me what he thinks.

Embarrassed, I take the coffee.

It's milky and steamy, which is exactly how I like it. I close my eyes, breathing in the deep aroma. It's comforting and familiar in a day that's been anything but.

When I open my eyes, Davis is staring at me in a way that makes my pulse beat a little faster.

"Danni said you'll be working here today. Do you have everything you need?"

I set the coffee mug on the table. "You got the WiFi password?"

"I'll grab it for you."

He heads to the bar just as Hercules pads into the room. The giant dog stops when he sees me and heads straight over, his tail wagging.

Davis intercepts him, but I wave him away. Who can resist a big goofy grin like the one I'm getting from Hercules?

"It's okay," I say. "I don't mind dogs. He just startled me this morning, that's all."

"And ruined your shirt. I'll buy you a replacement if it doesn't come out."

The big dog puts its head in my lap, and I run my hand over his soft ears. Hercules lets out a satisfied grunt.

"It's fine."

I don't want to tell Davis how much my shirt cost. I doubt a bartender would want to spend that much money on a designer shirt, and I don't want to embarrass him. Or me. He'll think I'm ridiculous if he knows how much I spent on this shirt. I got it on sale from an outlet store, and it still made my eyes water.

"It was old. I was going to get rid of it anyway." I keep rubbing the big dog's head so he doesn't detect the lie. "What kind of dog is he?"

"He's a St. Bernard."

Davis hands me the WiFi password on a piece of paper, and I enter it into my laptop.

Hercules whines when I take my hands off his head and licks my knee. The wet warm tongue makes me laugh.

"I love big dogs. I've never been able to get a pet."

"Why not?" He regards me curiously, and I keep my eyes on my laptop.

I don't want to tell him Jeff hates animals. And we weren't allowed pets in the apartment anyway. I kept pushing for a move to the suburbs with a backyard for a dog, but Jeff preferred the city.

"I live in the city," I say.

Davis nods, and I'm grateful that he doesn't press.

"I need to get the bar open, but shout if you need anything. I'm here all day."

"Thank you."

He tries to drag Hercules away, but the big dog refuses to budge.

"It's okay. He can stay with me."

"Are you sure?"

"I don't think I have a choice." I smile at Hercules as he settles himself under my chair, his huge body nudging the chair sideways. I don't know why this dog's taken a liking to me, but it's comforting.

"He likes you." Davis smiles, and it lights his youthful face up and takes my breath away, making my pulse race a little faster. I must be staring at him, because his smile falters.

"I'll be right here if you need me."

I like the way everyone here is carefree and easygoing. Not like the city where people are guarded.

His jeans hug his backside as he walks to the bar, and I smile to myself. This might not be a bad place to unwind for a few days. Get my head back in the right place before I return to the city.

3

DAVIS

I've never been jealous of a dog before, but right now I'd give anything to trade places with Hercules and have my head on Mel's lap.

She rubs him behind the ears, and he sighs contentedly. Lucky dog.

I tear my gaze away from Mel and pull the clean glasses from yesterday out of the dishwasher. As I put them away, my gaze darts to the woman in the corner.

The morning sun steams in the window, highlighting her hair in different shades of chestnut and caramel. The shiny tresses hang loose over her shoulders, and the tendrils snake down her chest. The white blouse, streaked with dirt thanks to my dumbass of a dog, hug her ample breasts. The top button hangs loose, giving a tantalizing glimpse of milky white skin a shade lighter than her arms, the most private parts of her body where the sun doesn't reach.

"Put your tongue back in your mouth."

I glance up, startled to find Charlie watching me. Her arms are folded across her chest and there's an amused smirk on her made-up face.

She's the Prez's daughter and a few years younger than me, not that you'd notice with the way she's taken to presenting herself lately. I'm not sure why, but ever since the Prez went on vacation to Italy with his wife and young family, Charlie's taken to wearing heavy eyeliner and skirts that get shorter every day.

I'm not sure what she's trying to prove, but I also know you'd be stupid to even look at the Prez's daughter. Not that Charlie is my type. We've become friends since she started working as a waitress, which is why I flick my dishcloth at her now and she easily dodges out of the way.

"I don't know what you're talking about."

She raises her eyebrows at me and glances over at Mel.

"Looks like your dog isn't shy about making a move."

Hercules sighs contentedly, and Mel gives him an absent-minded scratch behind the ears.

"Shhh."

I adjust my hearing aids, because I'm never quite sure if I'm hearing things amplified or not, but the last thing I want is Charlie shouting across the restaurant about how obvious it is that I can't keep my eyes off the pretty brunette in the corner.

"Relax." Charlie leans her elbows on the bar. "She can't hear me."

I make Charlie her usual coffee, which is a straight up black with plenty of sugar.

I wonder if it's that obvious to everyone that I'm attracted to Mel. Not that it matters. A woman like that would never go for a guy like me.

"Are you gonna ask her out?"

"Charlie..." I cut a glance at Mel, but she's busy at her laptop with an adorable frown creasing her forehead.

"Of course I'm not gonna ask her out," I whisper. "A woman like that is way out of my league."

Charlie shakes her head at me. "Don't sell yourself short, Davis. You'd be a catch for anyone."

I appreciate her trying to make me feel better, but I know that's not true.

"Yeah, women are falling over themselves to get to me, haven't you noticed? They all want a half-deaf twenty-six-year-old who works in a bar for a living."

I try not to sound bitter, but the hearing aids are a real buzz killer. I haven't even tried approaching a woman since I got them. Who wants a guy with ears like an old man?

Charlie takes a sip of coffee and raises her eyebrows at me.

"You mean they want a kindhearted veteran who sacrificed his hearing for his country, who rides a badass motorbike, has a cute dog, and works at a bar while he learns the ropes of running a motorcycle club? I told you you're a catch."

At that moment Barrels strides in, a scowl on his face directed at Charlie.

"Who's a catch?" he demands.

Charlie sips her coffee slowly, looking up at him from behind the mug. "Davis is."

Barrels turns his scowl on me, and I wonder what's got him so worked up.

"The kegs need changing, and there are dishes from yesterday that need putting away."

He's not usually so pushy, but maybe with the Prez away he's feeling the pressure of being second in command.

He turns to Charlie, who smiles sweetly as she taps the barstool with her foot. "And I mean it about that skirt. You get changed into something decent, or you're not working today."

Charlie rolls her eyes, but she stands up from the stool. "Fine. I'll put something else on. If you're sure you don't *want me* in this skirt?"

Barrels glances down at her legs and swallows hard. Charlie gives him an innocent smile and steps one booted foot onto the rung of the stool.

She's flirting with him.

The Prez's daughter is flirting with her father's best friend, and by the way he's breathing heavily, I'd say he feels the same attraction to Charlie that I do to Mel.

Well shit. This isn't going to play out well.

"Do you have any other WiFi, or is that it?"

The silky voice makes my head jerk up to the corner where Mel's forehead is puckered into a frown. "I've just done a test call with my PA, and the signal's breaking out on the video. I can't let my team know I'm not in Charlotte. They think I'm working from home today, and I don't want them to know I've escaped to the mountains."

There are worry lines on her forehead, and I want to smooth them out and make all her worries disappear. I'm not sure what's driven this woman to flee the city, but now that she's here I'll do anything I can to make her stay.

"Afraid not. Signal can be patchy out here in the mountains. That's why I got a Starlink satellite dish at my cabin."

She raises her eyebrows, and I love that I've impressed her.

I'm about to tell her that it's easy to move and I can bring it to the clubhouse when a better idea occurs to me.

"You want to go to my place to work instead?"

She tugs on her bottom lip, considering the offer.

"I'm just up the road. I can get you there in ten minutes. Still time to make your meeting."

I try to keep the excitement out of my voice, but now I'm running away with the idea.

"You could stay with me if you want. Danni's place must be noisy with the renovations and the kids. I've got a spare room and a quiet place to work."

I'm holding the dishcloth so tightly wrapped around my hand that I almost cut off my circulation as I wait for her answer. She tilts her head and wraps a strand of hair around her finger. I study her face and get the feeling that my entire future depends on her answer.

"Will this do?" Danni appears in the doorway of the

restaurant holding up a green blouse. "It needs an iron, but it's the dressiest thing I could find."

Mel crosses the room, leaving Hercules to look mournfully after her, and inspects the blouse. "That will have to do. I don't have many choices."

She takes the blouse and holds it up, shaking it out to try to get out the creases.

"I've got an iron at my place too," I say, reminding her of my offer.

"The WiFi's crap," Mel explains to Danni. "Davis has offered his place up to work."

"And to stay," I add. "I've got a spare room."

I say it causally as I wipe down another glass. "I could run you back there now before we open for the day."

I'll have to ask Charlie to cover for me with setting things up and Quentin will have my ass since he's in a pissy mood, but I don't care. I'll have Mel at my place.

Mel looks to Danni and I collect some glasses from the other end of the bar, giving them time to talk about me if they need to.

"Davis is solid," I hear Danni say. "You can trust any of the men in the club. I told Barrels a little about your situation, and you're under club protection now."

Mel takes a step back. "Club protection? What does that mean?"

"It means if that asshole comes here looking for you, he'll have to get past a bunch of hairy veteran bikers first."

Mel breaks into the first smile I've seen since she arrived.

"I like the sound of that. But it's only for another night or two until I can get myself back to Charlotte and figure out my next move."

She goes to gather up her things, and I try to keep my eyes off the confident way her body moves.

She's under club protection, which means I'll do anything needed to keep her safe.

4

MEL

"I've never been on a motorbike before."

Davis slips a helmet over my head, and the closeness of him makes me dizzy.

"I'll take it slow. All you've got to do is hold on."

His fingers brush my chin as he does up the strap, sending a zing of electricity dancing across my skin. My gaze slices up to meet his, and he's watching me with intense green eyes.

It's been a long time since a man looked at me that way, like I'm desirable.

His warm breath tickles my cheek, and I catch his scent of coffee and leather and fresh mountain air. It's a heady, masculine mix, and I breathe in deeply. Such a different aroma compared to Jeff and the smells of the city.

"Don't go too slow," I say. "My meeting starts in fifteen minutes."

He grins, and there's a boyish charm to his smile. I'm

not sure how old Davis is, but he's definitely younger than me judging by the lack of wrinkles around his eyes.

"No problem." He slides onto the bike and helps me get my leg over the back. "Hold onto me."

It feels less weird than it should to put my hands on this stranger's waist. The leather is cool under my fingers, and I cling onto the solidness of him.

Hercules is strapped into the side car with special goggles on and a big doggy grin on his face. I'm guessing he loves riding as much as his owner does.

We head out of the parking lot and up the mountain. The wind whips my hair behind me, and my heart hammers in my chest.

I can tell why they love to ride. The tension falls out of my shoulders, and there's nothing to do but cling onto Davis and admire the view.

It's a rush, and one that I'd never have in the city.

I've always taken the sensible path. I was a model student and went off to study economics at college. I got a job in the city and bought a safe car and got a safe boyfriend.

They were all things I thought I wanted. But as I cling onto Davis as he tears up the mountain, I wonder what I've been missing.

Too soon we turn onto a dirt road and a log cabin comes into view. It's like a cabin you see in the movies with round logs slotted together that meet in a peak in the middle. But it's bigger than I expected for a single man.

Unless he's not single.

The thought disturbs me more than it should, and I shake it away. It doesn't matter if this cute biker is single or not. I'm here for one or two nights until I can figure out new accommodations in Charlotte and get my stuff out of Jeff's house for good.

I follow Davis up the steps to the wraparound patio, trying not to notice the way his butt moves in his tight jeans.

Hercules pads behind, his paws clicking softly on the wooden stairs.

The cabin is as beautiful inside as it is out. The front half is open plan with a huge kitchen island surrounded by barstools and a long wooden dining table with bench seats.

On the other side of the room, there's a fireplace and an L-shaped couch that looks like it could fit a soccer team.

"Who else lives here?" I ask, not wanting to examine why my chest is tight while I wait for an answer.

"Just me," he says with a smile.

He gives me a quick tour, showing me the bathroom and where to help myself to food in the kitchen. Then he sets me up at the end of the long dining table where there's a power outlet.

I long to explore what's down the hall and all the rooms with closed doors, but my meeting's in a few minutes and I need to check the connection.

I get the laptop going while Davis brings out an ironing board and iron.

"You don't have to do that."

He gives me a stern look that makes my tummy do a little flip.

"You get your call set up, and I'll get your shirt ready."

I do a quick test with Alice, my PA and the only person who knows where I am today. I can trust Alice with anything, and I make a note to send her a box of flowers and cookies for her grandkids. A discreet PA is worth their weight in gold.

Everything's ready with a few minutes to spare, and I admire Davis expertly wielding an iron. I don't think Jeff has ever even done my laundry let alone ironed my clothes for me.

He takes it off the board with a flourish and hands it to me.

"Thank you."

I grab the blouse and head to the bathroom for a quick change.

I've got a stick of concealer in my handbag and lip-gloss, but that's all the makeup I carry with me. I pinch at my cheeks, trying to get color into them, and run my fingers through my hair.

For the first time, I wonder if taking off spontaneously straight from the office was the right move. But it's too late to go back now. I've got my laptop, a pretty blouse, and some lip-gloss. That's all I need.

When I come out, Hercules has made himself comfortable on the floor near my chair.

"Come on, Hercules, you're coming back with me," Davis says to him, but the big dog only looks at him with sad eyes.

"He can stay here."

"Are you sure?" Davis asks. "He's a lot."

Hercules turns his mournful eyes on me, and I rub him behind the ears.

"We'll be fine. Won't we?"

"I'll be back as soon as my shift finishes. Help yourself to anything you find in the kitchen and take a shower if you want. The first bedroom on the right is yours. I'll clear it out when I get back."

I'm so grateful for this stranger opening up his home to me that tears suddenly sting my eyes.

Davis looks horrified, and I blink them away quickly.

"It's okay. You've just been so kind, that's all."

I don't think there's anyone in Charlotte who would have taken me like this, yet this complete stranger here has.

Davis looks like he's about to say something, but at that moment my laptop chimes with the incoming video call.

"I'll call in a few hours to see how you're doing,." Davis says from the doorway. And then he's gone.

I watch him jog down the stairs and slide onto his bike, wondering what I can do to repay his kindness.

Then I take a deep breath and answer the call.

5
DAVIS

I've never ridden so fast up the mountain as I do that evening. As soon as the last customer leaves, I grab my keys and jacket. Charlie gives me a knowing look and chuckles, then offers to close up the bar for me. I owe her one.

I'm out of the clubhouse at a jog, then I'm on my bike and tearing home to Mel.

I kick up the dirt as I pull up outside my cabin. The smell of woodsmoke hits me, which means Mel figured out how to get the fire going. But when I open the door, it's the aroma of roasting chicken that has my mouth watering.

Mel's in the kitchen with her back to the door, singing along to Taylor Swift which blares from her phone. She wiggles her ass, dancing to the music and flailing a wooden spoon in one hand. When she sees me she stops abruptly and lunges for her phone to turn off the music.

Silence fills the cabin except for the sound of Hercules's claws on the wooden floor as he pads over to say hello.

"Keep the music on if you want." I don't add that I like seeing her dance, watching her body move.

I hang my jacket by the door and toe my boots off.

The steam from the kitchen has given Mel a soft look, heating her cheeks a healthy pink. It's the sight of her that makes my mouth water as much as the smell of roasting meat.

"I cooked dinner. I hope you don't mind."

She smiles tentatively, and I match it with a grin.

"Do I mind coming home to a home-cooked meal? Um, no."

It's been too long since I had female company and longer still since anyone cooked for me, apart from the club dinners every month. But this is different. This is intimate.

"I found the chicken in the freezer. I hope that's okay. I can replace it tomorrow."

She tucks her hair behind her ear, and I resist the urge to reach out and smooth the rest of it down for her.

"You don't need to replace it, Mel. You're my guest."

There's a pot of gravy bubbling on the stove, and she gives it a stir with the wooden spoon.

"Your timing is perfect. The chicken is resting, and the roasted vegetables are ready."

I set the table while she dishes up, making sure to use the best placemats and the wide ceramic plates.

"I don't have any wine, only beer. Do you want one?"

She nods, and I grab two beers from the fridge. If I'd known she was coming I'd have gotten something fancy, but she seems happy enough when I hand her the beer.

"I'll get you a glass."

She shakes her head. "No need. Just because I'm from the city, Davis, doesn't mean I don't drink my beer straight from a bottle."

I sit down opposite her, and my heart's hammering in my chest. I've never had a beautiful woman share my dinner table, and even though I'm in my own house I'm at a loss for words.

I tuck into the food instead, and the tastes explode on my tongue. Damn, she's a good cook.

"This is good," I say around a mouthful of chicken. "Moist."

Which isn't a great choice of words. But Mel murmurs a thanks, and we eat in silence.

The fireplace gives the room a golden glow, and I like the way she looks in my cabin. Like she belongs here on the mountain.

I wonder what it would take to get Mel to stay here. If she could ever live in a cabin like this away from the city. I shake the fantasy out of my head because that's what it is: a fantasy. I'm getting carried away by the first woman I've ever had over for dinner.

Now I'm regretting staying away from women for the last two years. I'm out of practice. I'm tongue-tied and feeling every bit the younger man that I am.

"Did your call go okay this morning?" I ask, trying to keep the nerves out of my voice.

She nods. "Yeah. They had no idea I wasn't in my apartment. I've worked from home before, and I just put on a generic background so they couldn't see where I was."

"Does it matter where you work from?"

"It shouldn't. But I've applied for a new position, and I don't want to rock the boat."

"Is it a promotion?"

She nods. "For an investment portfolio manager. This kind of role doesn't come up often, and it's the next step up for me."

I nod along as if I know what she' talking about. Danni told me her sister works in finance, but it's all too complicated for me.

"I'm not sure what that is, but it sounds smart."

She crinkles her nose up. "Most people don't understand the ins and outs of investing, which is what keeps me in a job. It basically means I'd be managing an investment portfolio, deciding where to invest people's money and when to invest and when to withdraw."

Damn, she's smart as well as beautiful, which makes her way out of my league. But she's here for a few days, so I can pretend I'm someone she could be interested in.

"Do you enjoy your job?"

She smiles and nods. "Yeah. To some people finance is boring, but I've always enjoyed it. I'm good with numbers, and I like the strategy that comes with it."

Her eyes light up as she tells me about her job, about studying at college and joining the bank as a junior analyst and working her way up to where she is now. It's clear she loves what she does, which means my fantasy of her staying on the mountain isn't going to happen.

But the way she lights up when she talks about it makes her even more attractive. Mel knows what she wants, and I've got no doubt she'll get that promotion.

We're in the kitchen washing up, and I've angled myself to wash so my good ear is to Mel, who's drying. My ears feel tired after wearing the aids all day, and I slipped the right one out earlier. It's my better ear, and I give it a rest sometimes but leave the aid in the left ear.

Since I got over my initial nervousness, we've talked easily through dinner. I've told her about my work, which seems completely uninteresting compared to what she does.

"The truth is the MC saved me. I was lost when I came back from the military. I thought that would be my career for life."

She runs the dishcloth around a plate and stacks it in the cupboard on top of the others.

"Why did you leave the military?"

There's a burnt-on gravy stain on the pot, and I scrub at it with the scourer.

"I was honorably discharged."

I don't like talking about my hearing loss and what led to it, and I'm not ready to tell Mel about it. The fact that I've kept my hearing aids hidden this long is a miracle, unless she's noticed and hasn't said anything.

"This one will have to soak." I slide the pan into the soapy water and turn the conversation to something else. "Do you want a hot drink? I've got hot chocolate."

Her eyes light up as I turn the kettle on to boil. "I can't remember the last time I had a hot chocolate. Probably not since I was a little girl."

She's smiling as she says it, but I can't help but kick myself. I don't want to remind her of the age difference between us. I don't want her to think of me as some kid.

"I keep it for when the kids come around."

Her eye widen in surprise. "You have kids?"

"No." I chuckle. "Not my kids, but there are enough rug rats at the club now that I keep some treats and kids toys for anyone who stops by. And that includes your wild nieces."

She smiles softly, and her hand rests on my arm for a moment. "That's sweet."

Her fingers tap my forearm, making the hairs bristle. I catch my breath, and our eyes lock. She's so close it would only take a slight lean in to reach her mouth with mine. My eyes dart to her lips, and she parts them slightly.

Then the kettle boils over and she takes a step back and the moment's gone. I'm breathing hard as I pour the hot chocolates. I was that close to kissing Mel, and the weirdest thing about it is I think she was going to let me.

Which just shows how vulnerable she is, if she's looking at me as a rebound. But I don't want to be Mel's rebound. I want more than that.

Mel settles herself on the couch, and I bring over the steaming mugs.

"Thank you for letting me crash tonight."

I hand her the mug of hot chocolate and take a seat on

the couch next to her. The fire crackles and in the golden light she looks majestic, soft orange light softening her features and smoothing out the worry lines.

"Stay as long as you like. I mean that."

She shakes her head. "Thanks, but I need to get back to the city."

Even saying the word makes her lips form a tight line, making me wonder what she's going back for.

"Do you?"

She glances up and me, and I push on. "I'm not sure what your situation is, and if you don't want to tell me that's fine, but from what I can tell, something made you run. And if you don't need to be in the office, why not work from here? I've got fast internet; I've got a spare room and the space for you, and I'll be out of your hair most days. You can take the time you need to process whatever it is you're running from."

She takes a sip of hot chocolate then makes a face when it's too hot. Setting the mug down on the coffee table, she turns to me.

"It's my ex," she says. "The thing I'm running from."

My eyes darken, and my fists clench. "Did he hurt you?"

"No." She shakes her head, and my muscles relax. "Nothing like that."

I keep my eyes on her, letting her speak.

"I left him actually."

I don't know why that makes me feel relieved, knowing she's the one that ended it.

"We've been together a long time. Engaged for the last

few years. But every time he tried to set a date for the wedding, I found a reason to delay."

I take a long slow breath. Whatever happened with this guy, it doesn't sound like she was in love with him. And that makes me feel better than it should.

"We work together, and he knew I was going for that promotion. Yesterday I overheard him speaking to my boss, telling him why he'd be the perfect person for the job."

"Ouch. He went behind your back?"

She nods grimly. "And it gets worse. He told our boss that we're trying for a baby, and I'll be pregnant soon and will quit work to look after the baby."

The thought of her having someone else's kids makes my blood heat.

"Is that true?" I try to keep the strain out of my voice.

"No." She looks horrified. "I mean, I want kids. But I'd still work when I have them."

My knuckles clench just thinking about this asshole.

"All this time he was encouraging me to apply for the position, to go for it. But the reality is he wants it for himself, and he's prepared to throw me under the bus to get it."

"Sounds like an asshole."

I'll never understand how beautiful, smart women end up with guys like that.

"So I walked out. Grabbed my laptop and purse and went straight to the train station. I've got no plan, no belongings. I just know two things. I'm never going back to Jeff, and I want that promotion."

"You want it to spite him?"

She shakes her head. "No. I want it because I'm the best person for the job. I'm great at what I do, and the work excites me. It's got nothing to do with Jeff."

Her eyes sparkle, and I see the truth in it. Mel wants that promotion. Even though that means she'll be staying in Charlotte doing a fancy job while I'm in the mountains bar tendering, I vow I'll do whatever it takes to help her get where she wants to go.

"What do you need?"

She tilts her head at me, confused.

"What do you need to do to get that promotion? Tell me, and I'll help you."

She twirls her hair around her finger, thinking.

"The timing is shitty. The first round of interviews are in a week, and if I do well I then need to present to the board of directors. I've got a presentation to prepare while my life falls apart."

"So you need a quiet place to get your presentation ready?"

"Yeah. I've been looking for hotels to stay in Charlotte until I can find an apartment."

I shake my head. "No. You're not house hunting until after you've secured the position. It's too big a distraction, too stressful."

She tilts her head. "Why are you interested?"

Because I'm falling for you. Because I want to see you succeed?

"Because it's obvious you want this, and you need to

focus on the job. Not on apartment hunting, or your asshole ex, or anything else."

She sighs and runs a hand through her hair. "You're right. But everything feels impossible right now. I've still got my day job to do, and I don't even have any clothes, and my boss thinks I'm about to go off and have a baby. It's a fucking mess."

She looks up quickly. "Sorry, I swear sometimes."

And she's fucking cute when she does.

"How well do you get along with your boss? Can you tell them that what Jeff said isn't true?"

She rubs her temples. "Pretty well, actually. Jeff thinks Peter is in the old boys' club, but I've always found him pretty fair. I get along well with his wife. She works too, and they share the childcare responsibilities, so I don't think what Jeff told him will throw too much of a wrench in my plans. But it's the betrayal of someone who's supposed to have your back that I can't get over."

"Of course not. Your ex is an asshole."

I can keep saying that all night. At least she agrees with me.

Mel smiles grimly. "I've been in denial about that for years."

"So can you have an honest discussion with . . . Peter, is it? And tell him that you've broken up with Jeff because of what he said. That you're committed to the company, but you need some time to work remotely to deal with the situation and prepare for the interview and presentation."

She chews on her hair thoughtfully. "And work from where? A hotel?"

I grin, because she's still not getting it. "Nope. Stay here."

"No..."

She starts to protest, and I cut her off. "I've got a spare room and the space. A satellite connection. And you're surrounded by woods and mountains to rest and recover for as long as it takes."

She sips her hot chocolate. "I need to think about it."

"Of course."

"All my things are in Charlotte."

"I'll get them for you."

Her eyes widen. "You can't do that."

"I can and I will." I'll make this as easy for her as possible. Show her what real support looks like. "I'll take the club van and a couple of the guys. You give me a list and a key, and I'll get your stuff. You don't need to see the asshole at all."

A smile spreads across her face, and she launches herself off the couch to wrap me in a hug. I'm engulfed by her feminine scent as her hair whips across my face.

"Thank you, Davis. Thank you."

I wrap my arms around her and pull her close. It's a friendly hug to show her gratitude, but when she pulls away, she doesn't move back on the couch. My eyes dart to her mouth, her chocolate-tinged lips.

I'm breathing hard, and my dick lengthens at her close contact.

It's been too long since I kissed a woman, and I can't

remember ever feeling this attracted to anyone before. But if she's just left her fiancé, then she's vulnerable. And if I'm inviting her to stay with me for two weeks, then she doesn't need me coming on to her the first opportunity I get and giving her more complications to worry about when she needs to focus on the promotion.

"I'll put more wood on the fire."

I stand up abruptly and move to the fireplace, wondering if I looked back at Mel now whether I would see disappointment or relief.

It doesn't matter. I need to keep my dick in my pants and not take advantage of a woman who needs a retreat. She's here in my cabin, and that's enough for now.

6

MEL

I'm awake at 6:00 a.m. the next morning, which is my usual get up time. I like to get to the office early.

But this morning it's birdsong that I hear outside the window rather than the sounds of the city.

I lie in bed, enjoying the feeling of not having to get up yet. My office is only a few steps away, and my first meeting isn't until 9:00 a.m.

I grab my phone and ignore the messages from Jeff. I allowed him one phone call when I first got to Danni's to tell him it was over. It's a decision that has been a long time coming, and there's nothing he can say that will convince me otherwise.

I search my heart for any regret and find none. The only thing I feel is a sense of freedom. The only regret is that it took me so long to leave him. Five years I was with Jeff, but I was unhappy for at least the last three.

I send him a quick message to say I'll stop by at some

point to get my things from the apartment. Either I'm going to stay here for a few weeks or I need to find a place in town.

My mind turns to Davis, the generous veteran with shy boyish charm.

Danni was right about the MC being like a family. He's taken in a complete stranger and offering me his spare room. I'll have to sort out an arrangement for paying him rent.

But first I want to speak to Danni for a reality check to make sure I'm not doing anything crazy.

There are also several messages from my mother, which I can't deal with right now. I've always been the golden girl, getting a college degree, a sensible career, and getting engaged to a sensible man.

I never had the pressure that Danni felt because she didn't fit the mold our mother expected. I fit the mold because it just so happens I enjoy my job, and at first there was something about Jeff that caught my attention.

I realize now his easy charm can turn on and off like a tap. After living with him for five years, I can safely say there is nothing charming about Jeff Simmons. And after he went behind my back at work, I have no regrets about leaving him.

I swing my legs over the side of the bed and pull on the sweater that Davis lent me. It comes to just above my thighs.

When I was younger, I used to try to hide my thick thighs, but as I've gotten older I give less of a shit what anyone thinks about my body.

This is who I am, and the shape of my body is only one aspect of me. If anyone wants to judge, they're too shallow to be worth my time.

I listen to the cabin creaking and the sounds of the winds rustling the trees outside. I've got no idea if Davis is an early riser or not.

Tentatively I open the door a crack and peer into the dim morning light. Down the corridor, there's a row of closed doors and I wonder what he's got behind them. It's a big house for a single man.

The warm smell of coffee reaches my nose, and I follow the scent to the kitchen. When I reach the doorway, I stop dead in my tracks.

Davis is in the kitchen wearing nothing but grey sweatpants. He's facing away from me, showing clearly defined muscles and a tattoo that runs down his spine in an elaborate interlocking design.

My mouth goes dry, and there's a tug in my core. My knees feel like they're about to give way, and I slam my thighs together to ease the ache that's building between my legs.

He reaches to a high cupboard for a coffee mug, and his bicep curls as he takes the mug off the shelf. I bite my lower lip, trying not to whimper.

It's been far too long since I was intimate with Jeff. And I don't think he ever made me feel this way just by reaching for crockery.

A moan escapes my lips and I clamp them shut, but luckily Davis doesn't hear me.

Instead I retreat a few steps, take a calming breath,

and thump into the kitchen. He turns when I get to the kitchen island, and my breath hitches in my throat.

His bare chest shimmers with perspiration, the muscles pulled tight from a workout. His dark hair is plastered to his forehead, and he sips from a protein shake.

"Good morning," he says cheerfully, flicking the coffee machine on.

His gaze travels down my body, which is covered by his large sweater, and stops when he gets to my thighs. His eyes turn an intense deep color, and he licks his lips before quickly bringing his gaze up to my face.

I tilt my head, enjoying his gaze on me. Davis is as attracted to me as I am to him.

The thought makes my tummy flip. It's been a long time since a man looked at me with desire, and I like it.

I reward him with a smile and lean on the kitchen counter.

"You're an early riser too, huh?"

He nods. "Got that from the military. I like to get up early and work out."

Which explains the sweat covered muscles.

"I hope I didn't wake you."

"I didn't hear a thing."

His torso is perfection. Tight abs glisten with perspiration, and there's a thin line of dark hair that disappears tantalizingly into the top of his grey sweatpants.

I have the sudden urge to lick the sweat off him just to find out what he tastes like.

"Help yourself to coffee," he says. "I'm going to shower, then I'll make you breakfast."

"You don't have to do that."

"I know." He takes a sip of his protein drink. "But I want to."

A little while later, I watch Davis climb onto his bike and head off to the MC headquarters. He cooked me scrambled eggs on thick toast washed down with coffee. I worried you couldn't get a decent coffee outside of the city, but that's not the case. Whatever beans he's got are dark and delicious.

I open my laptop, but my mind's distracted with thoughts of Davis's abs and the bulging biceps that could pin a woman down.

I can barely take in what my colleagues are saying at my nine o'clock meeting, and it's a relief when it ends.

Danni said she'd pop round sometime this morning, and I'm relieved when I see her Caddy pulling into the driveway. I need a distraction that's not work.

Even better, she's got the girls with her.

I meet her on the porch, holding out my arms for my little niece, Lucy. Bettie races up the stairs with all the confidence of a four-year-old wearing fairy wings.

"Are you staying in the mountains, Aunty Mel?" She hops on one foot in excitement, and I give Danni a quick glance.

"Just for a little bit."

She skips off into the house, and I follow her in. Lucy squirms in my arms, eager to follow her big sister.

I give her one last big sloppy kiss and put her on the floor. She crawls after Bettie, who's gone straight to the living room.

There's a wicker trunk in the corner, and Bettie opens it and starts pulling toys out. Davis wasn't lying when he said he has kids over. The girls seem at home here.

The thought makes me smile, and I'm struck again by how good Danni has it here with her extended club family.

I make us a fresh pot of coffee, and we sit at the table while the girls play in the living area.

"How are you feeling?" Danni asks, the concern obvious in her expression.

I take a deep breath, not sure of my answer. "I'm feeling relieved that I've left Jeff, I feel terrified about what happens next, I feel excited about the possibility of promotion..." I trail off, not wanting to say the last bit. And I feel attracted to the hot young biker who's taken me in.

Danni sips her coffee and looks at me long and hard like only a sister can.

"I'm glad you're not sad about Jeff. I never liked him."

"I gathered." My sister's usually the friendliest person I know, but she was always cool around Jeff.

"Davis says I can stay in his spare room for a few weeks." I sip my coffee, not trusting myself to meet her eye when I say his name. He's gotten under my skin, but everything's too jumbled up at the moment to know what that means.

But there's no escaping my sister's shrewd gaze.

"Good." She smirks. "It'll be good for you."

"Jeez Danni, I'm staying in the spare room. Not his bed."

She looks surprised. "I mean it will be good for you to stay on the mountain, get away from the city for a while." She laughs. "Why sis, what did you think I meant?"

I play with my hair, trying to hide my embarrassment. "Nothing."

She laughs again. "But if you want to stay in his bed, that could be good for you too. A little light relief might be exactly what you need."

"Danni!" My gaze goes to the girls, but they're playing with a doll and caught up in their own little world.

"I'm serious, Mel. Davis is a good guy, and he can't keep his eyes off you. You should consider it."

My cheeks blush, because I have considered it. I've considered it a lot since I saw his body on display this morning.

At that moment, Bettie runs over wielding the doll. "She works at a bank just like you, Aunty Mel."

Bettie jumps onto my lap, and her little sister isn't far behind. She whines to be picked up, and suddenly I've got two little girls on my lap.

The scent of milk and lavender soap fills my senses, and the smile I give them is all genuine. Bettie tells me all about the doll going off to work while Lucy bounces up and down making gurgling noises, desperate to speak like her older sister.

Danni watches us thoughtfully, and when the girls hop down, distracted by the next toy, I know what she's going to ask.

"I never understood why you didn't want kids, Mel. You'd be an amazing mother."

I sip my now lukewarm coffee and watch the girls.

"It's not that I don't want kids. What I realized recently is that I don't want kids with Jeff. He'd be a terrible father; he's got no moral compass, and our values aren't aligned."

Danni nibbles on a cookie. She found them in the cupboard and was as comfortable as her kids in making herself at home in Davis's cabin. "When did you realize that?"

I sigh heavily. "I've been thinking about it for a while, wondering why every time Jeff tried to set a date for the wedding that I had an excuse. I didn't want to be one of those women who stays with a substandard man because she's worried her biological clock is ticking.

"I realized I'd rather take my chances having a child on my own than have one with Jeff."

Danni's eyes widen. "You're having a baby?"

"No." I chuckle. "I mean, someday I'd like to. And I can't wait around too much longer. I guess that's part of the terrified bit. I don't know how my life is going to play out now."

Danni's lips pull up at the corners. "If you want some

practice making a baby, I'm pretty sure Davis will be willing to help."

I punch her playfully on the shoulder, and we both giggle. But I can't help wondering if she's right.

7

DAVIS

I pull the van onto the side street and maneuver her into the only parking space left. A car horn blares, and a man in a red sports car behind me shouts something rude because I have the audacity to keep him waiting for thirty seconds while I squeeze into this ridiculously tight parking space.

"You want me to go have words?" Arlo asks from the passenger seat.

I eye the angry man in the convertible through my rearview mirror.

"Nah. We're here to get Mel's things and get out. If we get distracted by every impatient dickhead in the city, we'll be here all day."

Arlo grins. "You're right."

He opens the passenger door and steps out, making sure the angry man gets a full look at the patch on his jacket. With his full beard and broad shoulders, Arlo looks formidable, and I'm not surprised the impatient guy suddenly remembers his manners.

With the van parked, I eye the apartment building, which is the address Mel gave me.

The building is clean light brickwork with white window frames. There's a bustling cafe on the corner and I can imagine Mel striding down the street in her heels, at home in a place like this.

We enter the building, and the concierge eyes us suspiciously. I guess two big hairy bikers wearing MC patches isn't a usual sight in this part of town.

"We're here to pick up Mel Malone's belongings from apartment 709."

His nose sticks in the air as he regards us. Mel told me she phoned ahead, so his disdain is only a formality. Arlo clicks his knuckles, but I give him a look. I don't want to cause trouble that might make Mel's life any harder.

"I take it you have a key?" His voice is as clipped as his attitude, and I'm reminded of why I hate the city.

I pull out the key, and we ride the elevator up to the seventh floor.

Jeff doesn't know we're coming, and I hope like hell he's not at home. The last thing I want is to run into Mel's ex and do something stupid like punch him in the face. From what Mel's told me about him, the guy's a jerk. Trying to get the promotion for himself by spreading lies about her is one major asshole move.

I push the door open, and luckily it's all quiet inside.

Arlo gives a low whistle as we enter the apartment,

his gaze transfixed on the view. The windows are floor to ceiling with a sliding door that opens to a balcony that looks out over the city with views of the river and park.

My feet sink into the plush carpet and I trail my fingers over the soft, expensive looking furnishings.

"Nice place," Arlo mummers.

It's a very nice place, and that makes my heart sink. The last few days with Mel have been amazing, getting to know her and trying unsuccessfully to keep my eyes off her. We've been talking and laughing, and I catch her looking at me sometimes too. My stupid heart thought a guy like me might have a chance. But when I take in my surroundings, the type of life she's used to, I'm reminded how beneath her I am.

There's no way I can provide anything like this for her. I've got a cabin in the woods and a slobbery dog, and until a minute ago I thought my cabin was nice. But this is something else.

"Come on," I grumble. "Let's get her stuff and get out of here."

I wheel one of the suitcases we brought with us into the bedroom. The bed is so big you could sleep a family of five in it. If Mel was my woman, I'd have a small bed so we'd spend the entire night cuddled together. With a bed this size, you could go a whole night without even touching each other.

Mel told me where we'd find her clothes, and I open the dresser by the window and start transferring clothes into the suitcase.

When I come to her undergarments, my hand trembles. I pick up a pair of black lace panties and immediately have a vision of her in them, lying back on my bed, her thighs parted.

"Stop daydreaming," Arlo says from the door, and I quickly stuff her underwear into the suitcase.

He's got a smirk on his face, which tells me he knows exactly how I feel about Mel.

"She still sleeping in the spare room?"

Arlo opens the wardrobe and begins transferring shoes into one of the suitcases. I take a blouse down from a hanger and carefully fold it.

"Of course she is. I'm not an animal."

He chuckles. "No, but you're a man."

I drop the blouse into the suitcase and reach for another, wondering if it's that obvious to everyone how I feel about Mel. "She's vulnerable. She doesn't need me hitting on her."

"Or maybe that's exactly what she needs." Arlo grins wickedly. "I've seen the way she looks at you, Davis. When a woman looks at you like that, she wants you to hit on her."

He chucks a pair of shiny red heels into the suitcase, and an image of Mel wearing them and nothing else flutters into my mind.

"I'm not good with women," I mumble. I hate the admission, but it's true. I don't have the easy charm that Arlo has. That's why his road name is Prince. Because he's Prince fucking Charming.

"You don't need to be good with women. You just need to be good with your dick."

I frown at his crassness. "Don't speak about Mel like that."

He raises his eyebrows at me and grins. "It's not just lust is it? You like her."

I fold another blouse, wondering how many of these damn things one woman needs.

"It doesn't matter what I like. I can't give her this…" I indicate the apartment "…can I?"

Arlo chucks in a pair of knee length black boots, and damn, this woman's footwear is giving me a boner.

"It may have escaped your notice, but it was this…" he waves his hand around wielding a sexy black stiletto, "… that she ran away from. So maybe an expensive apartment on the river is not what she really wants."

I don't know what she wants, but I doubt it's a young bartender who barely has two bucks to rub together.

We're zipping up the last suitcase when the door to the apartment opens.

"What the fuck?" A thin man in a grey suit wearing an angry scowl bursts into the apartment.

"We're friends of Mel's," Arlo says cheerfully. "She asked us to collect her things for her."

"Like fuck you are. That little bitch doesn't own anything here."

Anger flares inside me, and I stride across the room and grab him by the throat. His eyes bulge as I walk him backwards and pin him against the wall.

"You call her that one more time, and I'll throw you off the balcony and into the street."

Out of the corner of my eye, Arlo arches his eyebrows at me. I'm not a violent man and he knows it, but this asshole doesn't. If the people of this city are going jump to conclusions when they see two men wearing biker's patches, then I'll play to the stereotype.

"You're from that fucking MC her sister's caught up with, aren't you?"

"Got it in one, dickhead."

"Now," Arlo says cheerfully, "the last thing on her list is some items from your DVD collection. I'm not a fan of DVDs myself, prefer streaming. But if that's what the lady asked for, that's what we'll get her. If you can just show us where they are…"

Jeff is going red in the face, and when I unlatch my hand from his throat, he rubs at his neck.

"I'll get my lawyer onto you…" Jeff splutters.

Arlo spins slowly in the living area, scanning the cabinets. "I guess I'll find them myself."

He opens a cabinet and gives an exclamation when he sees the DVD collection.

"Get out of my apartment," Jeff growls.

"We'll just take them all then." Arlo grabs the stack of DVDs and chucks them into a bag.

"If I find anything of mine stolen or broken, you'll hear from my lawyer."

Arlo wheels out the first two cases, and I pick up the handles for the other two.

"You won't," I assure him.

"I'll speak to my lawyer anyway. We'll look into your club. Whatever dodgy stuff you've got going on, we'll find it."

"Don't you hate a stereotype?" I mutter to Arlo.

Our club's legit. We run honest businesses, but I'd be wasting my time explaining that to this asshole. There's only one thing I need him to know before we leave.

I stop before the door, and Jeff runs up against me. Before he can step back, I spin around to face him, grab his collar, and channel my best *Sons of Anarchy* tough biker dude persona.

"You come near Mel again, and I'll personally hunt you down and make your life not worth living. She's interviewing for the promotion, and if I find out you've told any other lies about her, I'll come back with my biker buddies to pay you a little visit. You understand?"

His eyes bug out of his head, and I take satisfaction in watching him squirm.

I leave the apartment with Arlo and the suitcases full of Mel's things. But the satisfaction doesn't last long.

I may have the brawn to protect a woman, but I'll never have an apartment like this. No matter how much I want to, I'll never be able to give Mel the life she's accustomed to.

For a blissful few days, I thought we might have had something. But I realize it's better to leave her be. Whatever attraction I thought we had, it doesn't matter. I'll never be able to give her what she wants.

8

MEL

One week later…

"Where do you see yourself in five years?" Davis pulls his face into a serious expression, and I press my lips together to keep from laughing.

"They aren't going to ask that."

He raises an eyebrow at me, staying in the role of interviewer.

"I don't know the 'they' you're referring to, Ms. Malone. But I'd like an answer."

I try not to laugh at the way Davis arches an eyebrow at me.

It's doubtful the bank I've been working with for the last eight years will ask such a standard question, but I guess I should be prepared for anything.

"Well, Mr. Whitlock, since you've asked such an original question, it will take me a few moments to think of an answer."

Davis's lips twitch, and I'm immediately distracted. Where I'd like to be right now is exploring how those lips would feel on my skin and running my hands over the abs I've been getting a peek of every morning once Davis finishes his workout.

It turns out one of the spare rooms is set up as a home gym and he makes use of it, grunting and sweating behind the closed door every morning and emerging looking like a Greek god in sweatpants.

Over the last week, we've settled into an easy routine. He rides off to work, and I stay here and work until he comes home in the evening.

Then we make dinner together, we take Hercules for a walk in the woods, and watch a movie sitting on opposite ends of the oversized couch. I've been on the back of his bike two more times when he took me up to the mountain to see the view.

But other than that, Davis has kept his distance ever since he came back from Charlotte with my belongings, which are mostly still in suitcases in his spare room apart from the clothes and toiletries I've needed.

It doesn't make sense to unpack when I'll only need to pack them up again when I leave.

The thought is like a lead balloon in my stomach, bringing me back to the present. To the man perched across the table from me pretending to be a serious finance man interviewing me as practice for the real thing tomorrow.

My palms sweat just thinking about tomorrow.

It's the first round of the interview process, and I'm doing it over video call. I came clean to my boss about the Jeff situation and where I was staying, and he was understanding which I'm grateful for. No more pretending to be somewhere I'm not which takes a load of stress off.

Jeff will probably use it against me when I'm not in the office for the interview tomorrow, but as long as I stay focused and give them all the reasons why I'm the best person for the job, then it shouldn't matter what Jeff says.

"I'm waiting, Ms. Malone."

The sound of my name in his low, guttural voice has a delicious shiver running down my spine. The problem I'm having is staying focused when there's a hot biker sitting opposite me and sharing my space.

My tummy does flips whenever I hear his bike coming up the drive, and when we're in the same room, I can't keep my eyes off him. Even now, my core's tugging in a way that's distracting, and I press my thighs together under the table to try to ease the pressure.

"In five years' time I'd like to still be with NC Finance. I love what I do, and I have a good working relationship with my colleagues. It's a progressive company, and there's no other financial institution I'd rather work for. I love working in the city, and I can't imagine leaving for anything."

There's a flicker of something in Davis's eyes, and he looks down quickly. Is that disappointment? It's been a fun week staying here, but I'll have to go back sometime. He must know that, and if he feels disappointed at the mention of my going back to the city, then why has he kept me at arm's length all week?

"You're ready." He pushes up from the table and heads into the kitchen with Hercules padding after him.

I gather up my notes and laptop and take them to my room. When I come back, Davis is in the kitchen chopping chicken pieces with the music playing.

I grab a knife and a cutting board and get started on the vegetables, automatically falling into our usual routine. It's a nice routine and comfortable, apart from the growing ache between my legs.

Later that night I lie in bed, listening to the branches scratching against the cabin walls. My body tangles in the sheets, and no matter what I do I can't get comfortable. I'm too hot, wearing too many clothes.

I need to sleep, or I won't be on form for the interview tomorrow. But every time I close my eyes, Davis's abs swim into my vision. I hear his hushed voice whisper my name, and lust consumes me.

My hands runs down my body over my clammy skin and between my legs. But it's not enough. I want to feel his big hands on me.

I'm sure there's an attraction between us, and I wonder if he's lying in bed aching for me the way I am for him. I don't know why he's holding back, why he doesn't make the moves when the attraction between us is so obvious.

Maybe he thinks I'm vulnerable, but we've talked about Jeff, and I think he understands that I was over him a long time ago.

Maybe it's because of the age gap. I've found out Davis is six years younger than me. Maybe that's what's stopping him. He thinks I'm too old. But the attraction I sense from him is real. He wants me, I'm sure of it, and I sure as hell want him.

Making a decision, I swing my legs over the side of the bed.

What's the point in being the older woman if you can't make the first move?

9

DAVIS

*L*ike I have every night for the last week, I find myself in bed with my dick in my hand.

It's pure torture having Mel stay with me. Blissful torture. I long to possess her, but it's more than that. She's smart and successful and kind, and everything about her is perfect. I want more than her body, but what does someone like me have to offer a woman like that?

So I've kept my hands to myself and let out my own release every night while thinking about her dark eyes and curvy body.

I'm lying in bed giving myself a long slow stroke when the door opens a crack.

Hercules has taken to sleeping in Mel's room and sometimes wanders around the cabin at night, so I don't think anything of it until Mel appears in the door.

Her mouth moves, but I've taken my hearing aids out for the night, and I miss what she says. It's impossible to read her lips in the dim light, but that doesn't stop me from staring at them.

"Are you okay?" I sit up in bed, and she steps into the room.

She's wearing an oversized t-shirt that rides up her thighs, and my gaze is drawn to the silky skin at the top of her legs. My already hard dick twitches at the sight of her.

She bites her lower lip, hesitating on the threshold. I don't want to ask what she's doing here, because I don't want to break the spell.

She steps toward the bed, and instinctively I open the sheets for her. Making some kind of internal decision, she climbs into my bed.

I close the sheet around her and she looks up at me, her eyes wide in the dark.

"I...um..." Her eyes dart to my lips, and I've never wanted to kiss anyone so bad. At this moment, I couldn't give a shit if I'm good enough for her or not. Mel's in my bed, and even I'm not naive enough to turn away a woman who climbs into bed with you.

My lips meet hers, and the way she yields to me makes me bolder. I slide my arm around her and pull her toward me.

I've been longing to touch her silky hair, and now my hand tangle in her tresses as I cup the back of her head.

Mel pushes onto her knees and slides one leg over me, straddling me and pining me to the bed. Her eyes widen in surprise when she comes up against my hardness.

I groan as she smiles lazily and wiggles her hips so my dick presses between her legs. Even through my boxers and her panties, the sensation makes me suck in my breath.

It's been too long since I was with a woman, and my body's on fire. I'm ready to lose it just from one touch, but I have to make sure this is what she wants.

"Are you sure this is what you want?" I can't tell if I'm yelling or not, but there's no way I'm breaking the spell to put my hearing aids in. "You've got the interview tomorrow, and with everything going on...."

There are so many reasons why we shouldn't be doing this. Her interview, she's just broken up with her ex, and she's far too good for me.

Mel smiles lazily and her lips move, but she must be whispering, because I can't hear what she's saying.

Frustration fizzles up inside me, but Mel leans forward and presses her lips to mine and her hips bump forward, showing me what she wants.

Her mouth moves around to my right ear, my good ear. "It's what I want, Davis. It's what I need." Her voice is husky, but I hear it. I hear her.

She leans back, one finger trailing down my chest, and I'm struck by the realization that she knows about my hearing aids. Of course she fucking does. She's a smart woman. She must have seen me taking them out or noticed when I don't have them in.

She knows and she didn't bring it up, and she's still sitting here on top of me giving me the sexiest smile I've ever seen.

Gratitude fills me for this woman who's come into my life. And whatever this is, I don't care. She needs me tonight, and I'll give her what she needs.

Mel angles her hips towards me in a slow movement, bumping her sex right up against my cock. My eyes squeeze shut as I try to hold it together. But without sight and with limited sound, the sensation from every touch is more intense.

My eyes fly open, and I grab her hips and pull her back. Otherwise, I'm going to lose it before I give her what she needs.

I take some deep breaths to get myself under control while Mel gently removes my hands from her hips and puts them above my head.

Holy fuck. I've never been with a woman who takes control like this before. It's so fucking sexy.

She leans in and nips at my neck, her hair falling over my chest and her scent filling my senses. My skin prickles where her hair tickles the skin, and I groan so loud I hear myself.

Mel's warm breath skates across my chest as she slowly kisses my nipples and traces the lines of my muscles with her fingertips.

My hips buck at the contact, and I don't know how much longer I can stand this exquisite torture. She releases my hands, and I slide them under her t-shirt and run them over the hot skin underneath. I reach her breasts and palm them, loving the way her back arches in response. Her eyes are half closed, and I can only imagine the moans coming from her lips. If I'm lucky enough to get to do this again, I'll wear my hearing aids so I don't miss a single moan.

I slide the t-shirt over her head and her breasts fall into my waiting palms, beautiful in the dim light, ripe and full, and I can't resist pulling the dark nipples into my mouth.

Her hips buck forward, and she grips my shoulder. But she steadies herself again and sits back, regaining control. And God help me, I let her.

She straddles me, majestic in her black lace panties, the fabric delicate against her pale skin.

Her hands run up my stomach, and I shiver at her touch. My abs tighten as she runs them over my muscles. I want to show her the best of me. I want to show her that I'm man enough for a woman like her.

I long to grab her hips. I long to throw her onto her back and lick her until she comes. But Mel has other ideas. And I let her do what she wants with me. She's worried about the interview tomorrow, and if this release helps her relax, who am I to complain?

Her hands slide down my stomach and to the top of my sweatpants. She releases the drawstring and exquisitely slowly pulls out my cock.

I almost lose it in her warm hand. She gives my cock gentle strokes, giving it the attention it needs. I put my hands behind the back of my head and watch her.

She presses herself against me, and my cock slides against the silky fabric of her panties. The wet gusset clings to me.

The scent of her is in the air, and pearls of liquid bead

at the end of my cock. If I don't get inside her soon, I'm going to lose it.

But this isn't about me. I need to make sure Mel is getting the release she needs. Although when she takes my cock and rubs it against her panties, the groan she lets out so loud I can hear it, it shows me Mel knows exactly how to give herself what she needs.

My hands slide down the back of her body, and I cup her buttocks. I start to slide the panties off her, but she shakes her head.

Without words she pulls the gusset aside, exposing dark hair and her glistening sex.

"I need a condom," I say.

Mel shakes her head and leans forward to my good ear again. "I'm on the pill, and I'm clean."

The thought of being inside Mel with nothing between us makes my dick jerk.

"I'm clean too," I say.

As soon as the words leave my mouth, she leans back and rises up on her thighs.

With my dick in her hand, she slides it up between her pussy folds.

I grip her buttocks, needing to hold on to something as the heat of her sears through me, making every nerve ending stand on end.

"Mel…" My own voice reaches my ears, and I must be fucking yelling now but I don't care. This sensation, this woman, it's almost too much.

Mel widens her stance and then slides onto the tip of my cock.

I'm engulfed by her, and it's the sweetest sensation I've ever felt. She slides down my shaft controlling the pace, her eyes getting wider with every inch. Her mouth drops open and her neck arches.

I grip the sheets to stop myself from exploding inside her.

Mel's panting hard as she slides down my shaft and I give her all the control, lying beneath her as she takes all of me into her body.

It's pure bliss and I want to stay this way forever, entwined with this woman who has my cock and my heart in her grip.

Mel rocks slowly back and forth, her mouth moving every time her clit bumps up against me. And damn, I wish I could hear properly the sounds she's making.

Her hands go to the headboard on either side of me, and she rocks back and forth slowly.

Her breasts fall in my face as she leans forward, and I capture them with my hands, taking her nipple into my mouth and sucking hard. Her hot breath skirts my good ear, and the moans and cries she breathes into my ear are a gift. They come in waves as she moves against me, taking complete control and taking what she needs from me.

The rocking gets more frantic, and I feel her building up to the release she needs.

One hand wraps in her hair and I bring her face towards mine, kissing her hard. She rocks against me, and my lips travel to her ear.

"Take what you need, baby," I whisper. "Take what you need from me. This cock is all for you."

The words elicit an urgent movement, and I hear my name on her lips.

She's clinging onto the headboard so hard I'm sure her knuckles must be white. With one hand in her hair and the other clasping her ass, I let her ride me until she breaks, peaking on my cock and screaming my name so I hear it loud and clear through the hazy quiet. As the orgasm washes over her I keep myself still, letting her ride out every part of her release.

Only when she opens her eyes again do I move, keeping a slow rocking motion. Her thighs tighten around me, and she takes over the rhythm until another orgasm crashes over her.

She cries my name into my ear, and it's too much. I grab her ass, and Mel gasps as I slide her up and down my cock.

Then I'm lost in her sweetness and tightness, my release exploding out of me with strong unrelenting waves that make me scream her name as I grab her to me.

We finish sweaty and satisfied, panting together.

As I hold her close, I wonder how the hell I'm going to get out of this unscathed. I'm not good enough for Mel. That's a fact. I'm not sophisticated, rich, or success-ful. But she's got a hold of my heart, and there's no denying it now.

10

MEL

I slide off Davis and into the bed next to him. He scoots down so our heads are both on the pillow and wraps me in his arms.

I have never in my life done anything as bold as what I just did, sneaking into a man's bedroom and blatantly seducing him. But it feels so freaking right.

We're lying facing each other, and in the darkness, his eyes are intense.

"I don't usually do things like that."

Davis squints at me. Then he reaches for something on the bedside table.

"I'll just put these in. I want to get every word of this."

It's the first time he's acknowledged his hearing aids. I get the feeling he was trying to keep them from me. Like I give a shit if his hearing isn't perfect.

He slides in the aid on the left ear and props himself up on his elbow.

"We'll have to do that again with these in so I can hear you moan."

A delicious shiver goes through my body that he wants to do it again.

"I said I don't usually do that."

"You mean come three times? Or keep your panties on? Because that's probably the sexiest thing I've ever seen in my life. Anytime you wanna do that again is fine with me."

His lips twitch up in a smile.

"I mean I don't usually sneak into bedrooms at night and seduce young men."

The smile slides off his face, and he lowers his eyes. I've offended him.

"Not that I notice you're younger than me," I say quickly. Because it's true. Except for the fact that his body's perfectly solid and seems to defy gravity in a way mine never has.

"How long have you worn hearing aids?" I ask, changing the subject.

He rolls over onto his back and looks up at the ceiling.

"Since I destroyed my hearing standing too close to an IED."

I rest on my elbow and trace the contours of his chest with my fingertip. He's too delectable not to touch.

"Thank you for your service. It sounds like you gave... a lot."

"It's a lot less than others gave that day."

He rolls himself back onto his side, and I take it he

doesn't like talking about it. My heart goes out to this man, serving our country selflessly and having his hearing destroyed because of it.

"Is that why you came to the mountain?"

"Yes," he says. "I have a cousin in King's County but no other family. It didn't feel right going back there when I was discharged. He's got a family and kids. I didn't want to be the sullen uncle."

"Were you sullen?" I find it hard to marry that with the easygoing, quick to smile man I've come to know.

"Oh yeah. I was a miserable bastard after I was discharged. Thought life wasn't worth living. I didn't think a woman would ever look at me with these things in."

I smooth the hair back from his ear and trace my fingertip around the device.

"You were wrong there."

He shakes his head. "No, I was right. You're the first woman I've been with since it happened, Mel. The first woman that I've wanted to be with since it happened."

The admission makes my breath catch. My chest squeezes thinking about how lonely that must be. A loneliness the kindhearted Davis doesn't deserve.

I want to wrap him in my arms and tell him he's not alone anymore. But I can't promise him that.

Before I can say anything, he rolls over and sits up.

"You better get some sleep. You need your rest for tomorrow."

He reaches to the side of the bed and grabs my t-shirt.

For a wild moment, I think he's going to kick me out of his bed and send me back to my room.

"You need to wear this for your own protection," he says, pulling the T-shirt over my head. "If I feel those breasts against me in the night, you're probably not getting any sleep."

With the t-shirt on, we snuggle down in bed. Davis pulls me close against him, and my head rests on his hard chest. The sound of his heartbeat soothes me into a peaceful sleep.

For the first time since I left Jeff and fled Charlotte, I feel relaxed and at ease.

I feel like I'm taking control of my life again, even if I don't know what the end destination is. All I know is right here listening to the sound of Davis's steady heartbeat is exactly where I need to be.

11

DAVIS

One week later...

I wake up to the jolt of the bathroom door closing. Mel's side of the bed is empty but still warm and I reach for my hearing aids, not wanting to miss her singing.

Sure enough, the shower's running and Mel's singing one of her favorite Taylor Swift songs. It's muffled by the wall that separates us, but I recognize the tune and her sweet voice.

I never thought I'd be a Swiftie, but two weeks of living with one has made me the biggest convert.

A smile crosses my face as I sit up in bed. The last two weeks have been the best of my life, and the past week has been phenomenal.

I'll never get tired of waking up with Mel in my shower, or in my bed, or in my arms, which is how I've woken up every morning since she climbed into my bed a week ago.

I don't know what this thing is between us. We haven't spoken about it, because I don't want to distract her from the promotion she's going for.

Mel passed the first interview with no effort, but today is the next stage. She's due in the office in a few hours to do a presentation for the board.

I've been running through it with her for the last few days. I know more about the financial markets then I ever thought I would and am in absolute awe of this woman who navigates them every day like it's child's play.

If I wasn't in love with Mel before, I sure am now.

The shower turns off, and a few moments later she comes through to the bedroom wrapped in a towel that barely covers her luscious body.

My gaze travels over her wet skin, and my cock springs to life.

"Sorry." She winces. "I tried to be quiet."

I check the bedside clock, and it's not yet 6:00 a.m. To get into Charlotte on time, I need to drop Mel at the train station at seven.

I offered to drive her all the way to the office, but she insists on getting the train. She wants to go over her presentation on the commute, which she can't do on the back of a bike.

I can't argue with that. But an uneasy feeling has been

growing in my gut about her returning to Charlotte. What if she never comes back?

Overcome by a sudden need to hold her, I climb out of bed and wrap my arms around her towel-clad body.

Her breasts press into my chest, and she sighs when she feels my boner rubbing against her.

"You got any nerves you need me to take care of?"

I nibble at her neck and she moans, her hips reflexively rolling against me.

"I wish there was time, but I have a train to catch."

She leans her torso away from me, but her hips linger against mine.

"There's always time."

I slide my hand up her towel, and before she can protest my hand cups her mound. The hairs are springy and wet from the shower and I rock her on my palm, putting pressure on her sensitive nub.

She closes her eyes and groans.

"Davis..." Her voice is breathless and needy. "I'll be late."

I slide a finger into her slick wetness and her hips buck forward, rolling onto my palm. She grabs my shoulders to steady herself, her actions contrary to her words.

"I'll be quick..."

"Exactly what a woman wants to hear..." she teases.

I kiss her mouth as my fingers give her what she needs. But it's not enough. She's about to disappear into the city, and when she sees what she's been missing, the flashy buildings, the expensive cafes, the men of business in suits with good jobs and fat wallets, she might forget about what we have.

I want to leave her with something to remember me by. I want to make her come so hard she'll have to come back for more.

Maneuvering her body, I spin Mel around and onto the bed, face first. The towel flies open, and she gives a yelp of surprise as I press down on her upper back and quickly pull her hips up toward me as I sink to my knees.

I spread her creamy thighs and press my mouth to her sex before she can wiggle away. Mel is a woman who likes to be in control, and I've enjoyed every blissful minute of that, but this morning, I'm calling the shots.

Her juices coat my tongue and I groan at the taste of her, fresh and clean and ready for me to dirty her up.

"Davis…"

Her words turn to a moan as I reach around and stroke the parts of her my tongue won't reach. A hand runs up her body and I palm her breasts, pulling her back toward me and onto my tongue. Her ass is in the air, and with my other hand I circle the puckered pink opening.

Her hips buck, and she gives a surprised gasp.

I smile and bring my mouth to her back entrance, loving that I can surprise her. Reminding her I'm not just some young buck who she's teaching to fuck.

The whining noises she makes tells me she likes what I'm doing. With my tongue and my hands sucking and nipping at all her sensitive spots, I slow it down until she whines my name.

"Davis… I want to come."

I chuckle, and the hot breath on her ass makes her shudder.

With my fingers inside her tight pussy and my tongue licking every hot spot I can find, I build up the pressure and the pace until she shatters around me, her pussy pulsing under my tongue.

"Davis!"

She screams my name, and I'm so glad I put my hearing aids in this morning. I love hearing every part of this.

Mel breathes hard and wiggles beneath me, but I'm not done.

I slide my boxers off and pull her hips up to meet my dick. She's so wet I slide right inside, making Mel cry out and grip the sheets.

I've never had her like this before. Every time she's been on top or writhing underneath me, but this is the first time I've had her on her knees. And she can't get enough. Her hips buck against me, and she reaches back to rub my balls between her legs.

But I want this to be memorable. I want to give her something she won't get from a clean cut city boy.

Her puckered entrance is glistening from where I licked it, and now I slowly insert a finger inside.

Mel tenses and I rock her gently, getting her used to the sensation.

"That feels odd."

I lean down and kiss her back. "Tell me if you want me to stop."

"No," she says quickly, with a whine to her voice. "I want you to keep going, Davis. I need you to."

I'd love to take my time and explore every new sensation with her, but I'm aware of the train we have to catch and my own need to possess her before she disappears to the city.

I slam inside, driving my cock home hard while my hands rub and caress and my finger presses inside her other entrance, making sure she's getting everything she needs and then some.

My balls pull up tight at the same time as I feel her on the brink.

"Davis…" she whines. "I'm gonna come."

"Come for me, Mel. Come now."

Her pussy grips my cock, and at the same time I pull my finger out of her back passage.

She screams my name, and her pussy grips me so tight I completely lose it.

Hot cum shoots out of my cock as I explode with all the force of a train wreck. Her hips buck and she cries out over and over again, the orgasm rolling through her in long hard waves.

My hands grip her hips, clinging onto her desperately, this woman I love, this woman I'm terrified to let go of because she might not come back.

Finally, Mel stops shaking and collapses on the bed panting. Her wet hair falls across her face and her eyes are closed, and I'm suddenly terrified I've pushed her too hard.

"Are you okay?"

She opens her eyes lazily. "Fuck Davis. No, I'm not okay." But there's a lazy smile on her lips. "I've never been..." Her eyes roll around in her head as she looks for words. "...fucked like that before. Never. That was... incredible."

I can't stop the grin from spreading across my face. "I'll get you a cloth."

I head to the bathroom and wet a washcloth. Then I carefully clean up the glistening residue that coats her skin.

My cum is lodged deep inside her, and that gives me satisfaction. Wherever she is in the city today, she carries a part of me with her, a reminder that I'm here waiting for her.

Mel sits up and pulls the towel around her.

"You almost make me want to skip the presentation and stay in bed all day with you."

She's smiling and my heart leaps, the selfish part of me ready to do just that. But it wouldn't be right.

Mel was born for that job; I've seen the passion she has for it in the last two weeks. I couldn't take her away from that her no matter how much I want to.

Besides, she'd get bored once the initial flash of hot sex has worn off. As much as I hate to admit it, the best thing for Mel is to get that job. I just hope I've given her enough to remember me by.

"Come on." I offer my hand, and she takes it and I pull her up off the bed. "You've got a train to catch."

Her gaze shifts to the bedside clock that now says

6:15. We've got forty-five minutes before the train leaves, and it's a twenty minute drive to the station.

"Shit." She leaps into action, the panic clear on her face.

I feel a pang of guilt for keeping her distracted but only a pang. She's got her clothes all laid out, and at a push I can cut five minutes off the ride.

"I'll make your coffee."

I pull on my clothes and head downstairs. While the coffee's brewing, I flash fry a piece of streaky bacon and an egg and make her a breakfast sandwich to have on the train. She'll need her energy for today.

Fifteen minutes later, we're on the road heading to the train station with Hercules in the side car and Mel on the back of the bike, her laptop stowed in the saddle bags.

We make it to the station with a few minutes to spare. Mel hands me my helmet, and I hand over her laptop bag.

It feels like a final exchange, like we've been pretending at a fake life for the last two weeks and it's time to drop the pretense and head back to our separate worlds.

Her hair blows in the breeze, and I scoop up a strand and tuck it behind her ear.

Don't go, I want to say. Stay here with me and my big dumb dog and make my cabin into a home.

But I can't say those things.

"You'll be great," I tell her, putting on a smile that I

don't feel. "You're made for that job, Mel. Remember that."

She nods. "Thanks for helping me prepare, and… thanks for everything."

Her eyes search mine, and there's sadness there. I wonder if she feels the same way I do about her, or if she's happy to get back to the city.

If she gets the job, she'll need to move back. We'll have another week together at most, but she's already been looking at apartments. I saw her on her laptop clicking through images of floor to ceiling windows, balconies with a view, and modern bathrooms and solid brickwork that probably doesn't creak in the wind and expand in the heat.

It's a world she belongs in, and it was stupid of me to think she might find happiness out here on the side of a mountain in the middle of nowhere.

Hercules whines, and Mel rubs his big head. "I'll see you tonight, big guy. Don't miss me too much."

The train rumbles into the station, and Mel picks up her bag. "Good luck," I say again, trying to keep it cheerful. "And here." I hand her the brown bag with her breakfast sandwich in it. "Bacon and egg. There's ketchup as well, so be careful how you eat it. I put a napkin in there for you."

She looks like she's about to cry, which is not the reaction I wanted.

"Hey, it's just a sandwich."

"Thank you. Davis, you're so sweet."

She pecks me on the cheek, and I smile because sweet

isn't what I want to be to her. It reminds me of how much younger I am than her. But damn it, I like taking care of Mel, and if I didn't pack the sandwich she might forget to eat.

The train door opens, and she steps inside. I watch her until she finds her seat and gets settled. She pulls her laptop onto her lap, and a look of concentration fills her features.

As the train pulls out of the station, she looks up quickly and waves, then turns back to her work.

I stand on the platform with Hercules until the train disappears around the corner.

Hercules whines, and I scratch him behind the ears.

"You and me both, buddy."

I'm happy for Mel to have this opportunity, and I've no doubt she'll kick ass with her presentation. But it's bittersweet. If she gets the job, she leaves. And I don't know if my heart can take that.

12

MEL

I wake the next morning as I have for the past week, tucked into the side of Davis. His arm slides around me and he pulls me closer to him, nuzzling into my hair.

I sigh deeply and shift my thighs so they press against his, enjoying his sleepy warmth.

I'll never get tired of waking up next to this man.

I squeeze my eyes shut tight at the impossible thought. The presentation went well yesterday. Better than well. I nailed it. I know I did. I spoke with confidence and parried all the questions.

But the board of NC Finance is a tough crowd. It was hard to gauge what they were thinking under their serious expressions. I'd hate to play a round of poker with those guys and girls.

I think I did well, but I can't call it. They weren't giving anything away.

Davis stirs, and I wiggle against him to let him know I'm awake.

"I'm not working today." He brushes my hair back and plants a kiss on the back of my neck that sends shivers all down my body.

I reach behind me and cup his already hard bulge in my palm. I don't speak. I don't think he has his hearing aids in yet, and I don't need words to convey what I want to do.

I love every one of his groans that come out of his mouth as I slowly run my hand up and down his length. For the next half hour, I don't think about the promotion. I don't think about returning to Charlotte. I lose myself in Davis.

"Did you grow up around here?" I ask as we hike through the forest a few hours later.

We've ridden to the other side of the mountain to hike one of the trails. The woods are thick with moss and undergrowth. Small creatures scurry away as we pass, and birds call to each other in the trees. My hand grips a bear horn even though Davis said they don't come this low down the mountain. I'm not taking any chances.

We had to keep Hercules behind today, because there are some parts of the forest where dogs aren't allowed.

"No. I grew up in King's County, mostly. With my cousin, Blake. His family took me in when my mom passed."

I stop walking and look at Davis. He's never mentioned his parents before, and now I know why.

"I'm sorry to hear that."

"It's fine. I was sixteen at the time. I moved in with my cousins for a year, then enlisted."

My heart goes out to the younger Davis losing his mother when he needed her the most. But he seems to have accepted it.

"Why did you come here and not go back to King's County?"

"I did at first. But Blake has his own family and little kids. I couldn't handle it straight out of the military."

He looks to me. "I was a miserable ass when I first got out. Retreating to the mountains and hiding myself away was all I wanted to do."

I reach out my hand and take his. He's making light of it now, but he must have been hurting to want to retreat here. A young man who should be enjoying his life hiding in the mountains--it isn't right.

"I served with Arlo, and when my career was cut short, he told me about the MC. When things didn't work out at Blake's, I came to check it out and never left."

My fingers brush against the bark of an ancient tree as we walk past. "They're like family to you."

"Yeah. They are."

Which is why I could never ask Davis to move to the city. It's clear he belongs here with the MC, with the forest, and with his big, stupid, lovable dog. And besides, he's six years younger than me. For him this is a nice diversion, but he can't be wanting the things I want in life. Not yet.

Because my time spent here with him, seeing Danni and the girls has awoken a need in me. They talk about the biological clock ticking, and for the first time I feel it. I want kids. I know that now. I wasn't sure before, but it turns out I just didn't want kids with Jeff.

The last few weeks have opened up my eyes to what family life can be like. And I want it.

But it's absurd to think this younger mountain man wants that too.

We come to a clearing, and Davis stops and slides the backpack off his back.

"This a good place for lunch?"

I take a seat on a fallen down tree, and he sits beside me. He pulls a brown bag from his pack and hands me a baloney sandwich.

We eat in comfortable silence. If I get the job, I'll be starting next week, going back to the city and leaving all this behind. No more comfortable silences, no more packed lunches, no more hot sex. And no more Davis.

My heart lurches at the thought.

I finish the sandwich, and he pulls two apples out of the bag. I take one, and my fingers brush the tips of his. An electric spark jumps off him and up my arm.

Damn, this man literally electrifies me. And maybe that's worth fighting for. I've always been someone who goes after what they want, and maybe if I tell him how I feel we can work something out.

Maybe if he feels the same, I could stay here and find

something else to do. I couldn't be a full-time parent. I love kids, but I need something else in my life. Maybe I could start a consulting firm or open a brand new business.

But my mind dismisses both those ideas. Because the truth is that I want the job at NC Finance. I want the job, and I want the man. But I can't have both. Or can I?

Maybe if I tell him how I feel, we can find a way. I'm not sure what that is, but if he feels the connection the same way I do, maybe this could work.

What's the point of being the older woman if you can't tell a man how you feel? I'm not a shy girl in her twenties, unsure and unconfident. I'm a badass thirty-something year old who's not afraid to go after what she wants.

I turn my body on the log so that I'm facing Davis, and he glances up at me. He must see the seriousness in my look, because his brow furrows.

"What's wrong?"

I open my mouth to tell him how I feel when there's a shrill noise from the pocket of my jacket.

I grab my phone, and the number is from the office. It's unusual to get a call on a Saturday, but I take it.

"This is Mel."

It's the CEO himself calling. I stand up and press the phone to my ear as excitement tingles through my body.

He tells me I've got the job, and I give a little jump and fist pump the air. A huge grin spreads across my face as I get all the details, then end the call.

Davis is watching me, and there's excitement in his eyes too.

"You got it?"

"I got the fucking job!" I squeal.

He jumps off the log and spins me around, letting out a long whoop.

"I knew you'd do it, Mel. I knew you'd get it."

His excitement almost matches mine, and I love how supportive he is of me. But it answers the question I was harboring. This is obviously a fling for him, nothing more. He's excited I've got the job even if that means I'll be leaving.

Happiness for the promotion gushes over me, but it's tinged with sadness.

"When do you start?" he asks.

"They're sending over the contract today. They want me in the office on Monday to sign it and start straight away."

He gives me a wide grin, but his eyes dart to the ground.

"Well done, girl," he says quietly.

He kisses me tenderly, and I kiss him back. We have one more weekend together. One more weekend, and then we both go back to our regular lives.

13

DAVIS

$\mathcal{M}$onday morning comes too soon, and I'm back at the train station seeing Mel off. She insisted on taking the train again into the office. Her suitcases are packed up and in my spare room until she finds somewhere permanent to live.

The entire weekend I kept her by my side, not wanting to waste a single moment of time with her.

My heart's been in turmoil, wanting to tell her how I feel but knowing it's pointless. She's heading back to the city, back to her career and her real life.

I was just a mountain fling. A way to let off steam for a few weeks.

Only it doesn't feel like that. The moments we've shared, the intimacy, the late nights talking and laughing and making love. It feels real to me.

We wait in the train station with my hands grasped in hers until the steady clacking of the train signals its arrival.

I turn to Mel and tilt her chin up to look at me. Her eyes are wet, and my heart jolts. Maybe she does feel this connection that we've got.

"Thank you, Davis. For everything."

Her hands sweep over my hair, pulling it off my face and tucking the unruly mop behind my ears.

"You shouldn't hide these," she says. "Be proud of who you are. You got them serving your country. You should be proud of that."

The gesture makes my heart squeeze, and I grasp her hands again.

I love you, I want to say. But what good would it do? Even if she does feel the same, our situation is impossible. She has a life in the city. My life's on the mountain.

The train lets out a heavy sigh and the doors slide open but still we cling to each other, neither wanting to let go.

But I have to let her go. I have to let her go and live the life she was made for.

I step back and unclasp her hands.

"You'd better go."

"Yeah." She wipes at her eyes. "I'd better."

Hercules nuzzles her hand, and she crouches down to whisper a few words to him.

Then she crosses the platform and boards the train.

Hercules whines and walks after her, and I have to hold his collar to keep him back. He lets out a bark as the train door slides closed.

Mel takes a seat by the window and holds up her hand for a final wave as the train begins to move.

Hercules moves uneasily, whining and pulling until the train leaves the station and disappears down the track.

We walk back to the bike, and Hercules gives me a doggy scowl as if it's my fault she's gone.

"I'd keep her if I could," I tell him. "But sometimes you have to let the ones you love go."

He growls at me, not buying it.

The cabin is silent when I arrive home. Hercules muscles passed and heads straight to Mel's room. Not that she slept there at all in the last week, but it still smells of her floral scent.

He climbs onto the bed, and I don't have the heart to kick him off. He lies down with his big head resting on his front paws and lets out an unhappy sigh.

I grab a coffee and slouch on the couch, feeling the same way as my dog. It's only been a few hours, but I miss Mel. I miss her presence in my cabin. I miss her wit and laughter and her passion for her job. I miss her body and her soul and the long chats we had deep into the night.

My phone vibrates and I grab it, my heart leaping thinking it might be her.

But it's Blake, my cousin.

Hey buddy, Everly's pregnant again. A boy this time.

I let out a long sigh. I'm happy for my cousin, I really am, but I'm sad at the same time. I want what he has. A family, a woman to love, kids of my own. I want that more than anything.

That's why I built a big cabin. I want to fill it with family.

Congratulations dude. You're gonna need a bigger house!

He sends back a laughing emoji.

Come visit us soon

I leave my phone on the couch and lean back, closing my eyes. I long for the type of family my cousin has.

When I got back from the military, he was settling down with Everly.

I stayed with him for a few weeks, but it felt too intrusive. He's a firefighter on shift rotation, and at the time he had two young kids and a baby. I was a broken man who couldn't sleep at night and was angry at the world for my hearing loss.

I hated bringing that energy into my cousin's happy home.

So I moved on, and I found the MC and my new family.

And if I moved on once, I can move on again...

Something catches in the sun from the window, and I pick up a strand of Mel's long hair. I've been finding it all around the house. Her damned hair gets everywhere.

I wonder how long it will be before I don't find her hair anymore. Before every trace of her is erased from my cabin.

The thought opens a new hole in my heart. A few weeks from now, all trace of Mel will be gone. It'll be back to me and Hercules and the MC.

Is that really what I want?

I sit up, suddenly alert as the idea takes shape.

If I started over once, I can do it again. The city will be an adjustment, and finding an apartment that takes Hercules will be difficult, but I'll do it for Mel.

I'll get a job, any job, something respectable in an office. And if she wants kids, I'll stay at home and look after them so she can have her career.

I haven't imagined this connection. I'm sure she feels the same about me.

And if don't tell her how I feel, she'll never know. She'll never know that I'll do anything to be with her. I'll move to the city, shave my beard, and work as a paper pusher in a shitty office if I have to. Whatever it takes, whatever she needs. I'm there for her.

I grab my jacket and the keys and go into her old room.

Hercules looks up at me expectantly.

"Come on, boy." He barks once and springs off the bed in a rare energetic spurt that seems to only happen when Mel's involved. "Let's go get our woman."

14

MEL

I practically dance out of the office building I'm that excited. The contract is signed. I negotiated hard, and I got everything I wanted.

I've met my new team, and they're a passionate bunch of people. Well, as passionate as financial analysts get. I insisted on taking Alice with me and giving her a promotion to executive assistant and a pay raise to match.

There were a few other conditions I insisted on, and I can't believe they agreed. I need a celebratory bagel, and then I'm calling Davis to tell him all about it.

My feet falter as I hit the pavement, because I don't need to call Davis. He's standing right there in front of me.

All six foot something of him in a leather jacket and beard, leaning against his bike with Hercules in the side car, a big lopsided doggy grin on his face. People are staring at the sight of the rugged biker in the city and his oversized dog.

"What are you doing here?"

My heart jumps in my throat, hoping he'll say he came for me.

"Mel..." He takes my hands and pulls me toward him. I fall into his arms, so familiar and sturdy. "I'm not gonna let you go like that. You belong with me."

I take a sharp intake of breath. His words are everything to me, answering the need in my very soul for this man.

"I know I'm younger than you and I work in a bar and I'm half deaf and broken, but I can change."

I open my mouth to speak, but he presses a finger to my lips and rushes on.

"I'll move here. I'll get a respectable job. I'll be your house husband if you want kids. Whatever you need me to do, I'll do it, Mel, because I love you and I don't want a life without you in it."

My heart swells at his words, and sweet relief rushes over me. The connection was real, and I didn't just stake my career on it.

"First of all, you're not broken and you don't need to change and you don't need a different job. You're perfect just the way you are, Davis."

Relief floods his face, and he smiles at me. I grin broadly, thinking of all the possibilities open to us.

"But you don't belong in the city, Davis." His face falls, and I run on quickly before he gets the wrong idea. "You belong in the mountains, and I belong there with you."

He shakes his head. "No, Mel. I can't let you give up your career. It's too important to you."

I grab his hands and pull them up to my chest, unable to contain my excitement.

"I don't have to. That's what's great about being fucking awesome at my job. I've negotiated to work from home permanently."

He stares at me, taking in what I've said. "You mean you're staying on the mountain?"

"Yes. I can do my job from home; I've proven that in the last two weeks. I just need to be in the office once a month for two days for board updates and to see my team. But I can do all the rest remotely."

He stares at me and I grab his cheeks in my palms, squeezing his delicious face and leaning in close so he hears every single word of this. "I love you too, Davis, and I want to stay with you. If you'll have me."

Realization finally dawns, and he sweeps me into a bear hug that lifts me right off the ground.

"You're damn fucking straight I'll have you, in every position in every room."

We're drawing a crowd, and I don't care. I can't get the grin off my face.

"And I've negotiated an extended maternity package, so when you're ready…"

He drops me abruptly to my feet and draws back to look at my face.

"I'm ready now, baby. I'll start our family right now if you want. Why do you think I've got such a big cabin? I want to fill it with babies. All those spare rooms, the big furniture? It's for the kids we're gonna have."

I smile at this man who's ready to give me everything I never knew I wanted.

Hercules jumps out of the sidecar and jumps up, one paw on each of us, wanting to be included. He licks my face, and I kiss his wet nose.

We've already started our family with this big cuddly dog. I don't even care about the prints he's leaving on my shirt or the crowd that's gathered to watch.

Davis kisses me and I give in to him, melting against him.

I've always been a girl who goes after what I want, and I'm damned lucky to get it. My career, a lovable dog, and my wild mountain man.

EPILOGUE

DAVIS

Six years later...

"Shhhh!" yells Tilly, with a scowl on her face as intense as only a four-year-old's scowl can be. "The movie's about to start!"

Her little sister stares at her defiantly and carries on bashing away at the xylophone as only a two-year-old can.

I resist the urge to slip off my hearing aids and instead scoop Jessica into my arms and tug the xylophone mallets out of her surprisingly strong grasp.

I carry her to the couch and take a seat next to Hercules. He doesn't even bother to raise his head, just lets out a sigh like he's got the weight of the world on his doggy shoulders. I squeeze in next to him and Jessica wiggles into my lap, getting comfy as if I'm the couch.

I don't mind at all. I kiss the top of her soft head, the wispy dark strands just like her mother's.

"I'm coming," calls Mel from the kitchen. "Start without me."

Tilly pushes the play button on the remote, and the theme song from the latest Paw Patrol movie starts.

She jumps off the couch to dance and Jessica follows her, and the work I've done to settle them down is lost.

My bones are weary from the early mornings with Tilly, who's never been a good sleeper, and the interrupted nights from Jessica who's taken to climbing into our bed in the night. Sometimes I wake up to find all of us in there and even Hercules sprawled across my feet.

I don't mind not getting much sleep, but Mel's pregnant again and needs the rest.

My beautiful wife sashays over from the kitchen and places the mugs of hot chocolate on the coffee table. She takes one of Tilly's hands and one of Jessica's, and they dance around to the music.

I'm exhausted and my brain feels numb, but there's only one thing to do when your family's dancing in the living room.

I pull myself off the couch and join them.

Jessica giggles and reaches her chubby hands out for me. I scoop her up by the waist, and she squeals as I spin her into the air.

Tilly wants a turn, and suddenly I've got two little girls clinging to me as I twirl around the cabin.

The spontaneous dance party has made them friends again, and this time when we take our places on the couch the two girls sit together, which means I have the rare opportunity to snuggle up with my wife.

"Did you get your prep work done?" I ask as she leans her head against my chest.

"Most of it. Thank you for doing dinner."

I kiss her on the top of her head. "Anytime."

In the last six years Mel's excelled in her job, moving up to the position of hedge fund manager. She's just as passionate about her career as she was when I met her, and I'm just as happy to support her in whatever capacity she needs.

She was able to take time off when she had both the girls, but when she was needed back in the office, I took up the bulk of the childcare.

It's been a special few years, and I wouldn't change it for the world. I love seeing my girls grow up. It's hard work but as any parent knows, the smiles and cuddles and giggles more than make up for it.

Besides, I have all the support from the club. Most days I bring the girls in, and they play with whichever other kids are around. Sometimes I drop them with Danni or Trish, and sometimes I have all the kids here. We help each other out raising our kids. The MC is the village.

Barrels said it was time for me to move on from the bar anyway and I've been helping him with the management of the brewery, learning about stock ordering and product supply and generally helping him out with the running of the place. There's a lot of flexibility, which is perfect for a working parent.

It's not long before Jessica crawls right over Hercules and onto Mel's lap. Another few minutes, and I've got Tilly on mine.

The girls are glued to the movie even though we've watched it at least twenty times before.

With an arm around Mel and another around Tilly, I let my head droop back. The crackle of the fire is soothing, and with the warm bodies around me a sense of contentedness fills me.

When I left the military, I doubted I'd ever have this life. But Mel taught me I was worth loving, and I'm grateful for that every day of my life.

The fire crackles in the grate and my girls giggle at the antics on the TV, Hercules's soft snores reach my ears, and Mel's warm body and sweet scent permeate my senses.

Parenting is tiring, and a happy exhaustion washes over me. It's not long before I drift off into a contended sleep. I've become the dad who dozes on the couch, and I couldn't be happier.

* * *

BONUS SCENE

Not ready to day goodbye to Mel and Davis? See what life is like for them in the future and if Mel has any regrets about the life she chose on the mountain. Read the Wild Love bonus scene when you join the Sadie King email list.

To get the bonus scene visit:
authorsadieking.com/bonus-scenes

Already a subscriber? Check your last email for the link to access all the bonus content and free books.

ALSO MENTIONED IN THIS BOOK...

Curious about Blake and Everly? Read their story in Blake, a firefighter and curvy girl instalove romance.

She wants to be an independent badass woman. He's the fireman lovestruck by her feisty attitude and goddess-like curves. One embarrassing rescue will change everything.

Blake

When we take the call to rescue a damsel in distress, I've got no idea that my life is about to change.

As soon as I see the curvy goddess standing on the roof, I know she's the one for me.

She's fiery as hell and fiercely independent with curves that are driving me crazy.

She says she doesn't need rescuing, but I'll do anything to be her hero if only she'll let me.

Everly

I've finally moved into my very own apartment and found the independence I've been craving. But getting stuck on the roof is not the badass maneuver I was planning.

I'm not going to go gooey over some guy just because he rescues me and is wearing a fireman's uniform, only my heart and my body seem to have other ideas.

But is he worth giving up my independence for?

Do you love firefighter romance books? Then the *Kings of Fire* series is for you! Smoking hot tales of insta-love, featuring brave heroes and sassy heroines that will melt your heart.

Blake is book one in the *Kings of Fire* series. Each book is a standalone, no cliff-hangers and always with a happily ever after.

BOOKS & SERIES BY SADIE KING

Wild Heart Mountain

Military Heroes

Kobe brings together a group of military veterans who live on the side of Wild Heart Mountain. Can these wounded warriors find love or do their scars cut too deep?

Wild Riders MC

This group of ex-military bikers fall hard and fall fast when they encounter the curvy women who heal their hearts.

Knocked Up

A side story to the Wild Rider's MC. A secret baby romance featuring an ex-military demolition man who thinks he's not worthy of love.

Mountain Heroes

Steamy stories featuring the men and women from Wild Heart Mountain's Search and Rescue and Fire service.

Temptation

A damaged hero and a lost virgin in an explosive instalove retelling of the Hansel and Gretel story set in the woods of Wild Heart Mountain.

A Runaway Bride for Christmas

A snowstorm keeps this runaway bride trapped in the cabin of the mountain's biggest grump.

A Secret Baby for Christmas

Mr. Porter's Christmas takes a surprise turn when his daughter's best friend turns up with his baby.

Sunset Coast

Underground Crows MC

Short and steamy MC romance stories of obsessed men and curvy girls.

Sunset Security

A security firm run by ex-military men who become obsessed with their curvy girls.

His Christmas Obsession

A Christmas romance about an obsessed biker who rides across the country in the snow to reach Cleo before he's even met her.

Men of the Sea

Super short and steamy tales from Temptation Bay of bad boys and curvy girls.

Love and Obsession

A bad boy trilogy featuring a thief, a henchman and an ex-military hitman who finds redemption with his curvy girl.

His Big Book Stack

The Underground Crows are called in to help an old friend do some digging when the woman he's obsessed with is threatened.

Maple Springs

Small Town Sisters

Candy's Café

All the Single Dads

Men of Maple Mountain

All the Scars we Cannot See

What the Fudge (Christmas)

Fudge and the Firefighter (Christmas)

The Seal's Obsession

His Big Book Stack

For a full list of Sadie King's books check out her website

www.authorsadieking.com

ABOUT THE AUTHOR

Sadie King is a USA Today Best Selling Author of contemporary romance novellas.

She lives in New Zealand with her ex-military husband and raucous young son.

When she's not writing she loves catching waves with her son, running along the beach, and drinking good wine with a book in hand.

Keep in touch when you sign up for her newsletter. You'll snag yourself a free short romance and access to all the bonus content!

authorsadieking.com/bonus-scenes

Printed in Great Britain
by Amazon